Flocks Of Birds

Flocks Of Birds

By Charlotte Zolotow

Pictures by Joan Berg

Abelard=Schuman
London New York Toronto

The little girl was already in bed
and her mother had kissed her good night.
"But I'm not sleepy," the little girl said.
"Lie here in the dark," said her mother,
"and think your thoughts until you are."
"Give me something good to think about,"
the little girl said, holding her mother's hand.

"Think of flocks of birds," her mother said.
"Close your eyes and think of flocks of birds
flying south."
"What shall I think about them?"
the little girl asked.

"Oh," said her mother, "think of a
dark meadow
in the mountains far away.
"The long black grass is filled with
sleeping birds.
"Think of the early morning light beginning,
and as the mist rises from the marsh,
the birds begin to stir.
"By ones, by twos, by threes, the birds rise up
circling above the meadow and the marsh.
"There is only one cry from one bird
as they begin their flight across the mountain,
over the valleys, over the ocean far below.

"Think of the sun which suddenly comes
through the clouds like a pale orange ball.
"The birds fly over the water, over the silvery sand,
over the city where people are hurrying
through the autumn wind on their
way to work.

"They fly on, over towns where the littlest children
swinging on swings in the early morning
tilt their heads backwards
and see the birds high above them in the sky.

"Through the morning, through the afternoon,
they fly over country fields bright with goldenrod,
over farms nestling in the browning hills.

"Now a school bus empties out the children
on a dusty lane and high above
the birds are flying, flying.

"They fly over mountains where the trees
are yellow and crimson and brown,
and only the pines are green.

"They pass over rivers where the boats cut
choppy little white-edged waves into
the windy water.

"And as the long afternoon light begins
to lengthen, they fly across a hazy white
shape that is the late afternoon moon.

"They fly through the long purple and
pink clouds of the sunset and through
the gathering blackness of the night.

"In the town far below them, lights go on like little stars in kitchen and living room windows. No one hears the sound of the birds passing high above in the dark sky.

"They fly across the huge harvest moon,
and over lakes where the water is like
a pool of black ink holding the moon's reflection,

and two deer stand side by side, drinking
at the water's edge.

"And the birds fly on and on over another small town where the houses are dark and little girls like you are sleeping, dreaming of lovely things

like flocks of birds
flying through the night
in the fall."